HORVOS
THE HORROR BIRD

With special thanks to Michael Ford

www.sequestbooks.co.uk

ORCHARD BOOKS

First published in Great Britain in 2014 by Orchard Books
This edition published in 2016 by The Watts Publishing Group

3 5 7 9 10 8 6 4

Text © 2014 Beast Quest Limited.
Cover and inside illustrations by Artful Doodlers with special thanks to Bob and Justin
© Orchard Books 2014

Illustrations copyright Orchard Books, 2014

Series created by Beast Quest Limited, London

A CIP catalogue record for this book is available from the British Library.

ISBN 978 1 40832 865 1

Printed in Great Britain by Clays Ltd, Elcograf S.p.A.

The paper and board used in this book are made from wood from responsible sources

Orchard Books
An imprint of Hachette Children's Group
Part of The Watts Publishing Group Limited
Carmelite House, 50 Victoria Embankment, London EC4Y 0DZ

An Hachette UK Company
www.hachette.co.uk
www.hachettechildrens.co.uk

HORVOS
THE HORROR BIRD

BY ADAM BLADE

ORCHARD

I'm coming for you, Max!

You think you have defeated me -
the mighty Cora Blackheart? Idiot
boy! You've only made me angry!
I may have lost my ship and my
crew, but it's not over. Now it's
just you and me...and the deadly
Robobeasts under my control!

You have something that I want, Max
- an object so powerful, I can use
it to rule all of Nemos! And you
don't even know it...

But first I will destroy your
whole family - your mother, your
father...and that irritating Merryn
girl, too.

Cora Blackheart will have her
revenge!

CHAPTER ONE

HIDDEN WRITING

Max crouched under the *Leaping Dolphin*'s main control panel at the front of the sub, trying to fix some damaged wiring. Two battles with Cora Blackheart's Robobeasts had taken their toll, but he was almost finished when a banging on the sub's screen made him look up. His Merryn friend Lia was swimming just outside the sub on Spike the swordfish. She laid her webbed fingers against the glass. Her skin was purple with cold and her teeth chattered as she

spoke through the communicator.

"Can't we get moving?" she asked. "It's freezing out here!"

Max glanced at his mother, who was reading a screen full of graphs and figures. She nodded. "Systems look good," she said. "Not quite back to full power, but almost."

Max slid into one of the pilot seats. "You could come inside," he said to Lia.

Lia rubbed her hands together to warm herself. "No way," she said. "You know I don't like travelling around in a big metal box. I'll stick to open water, thanks."

"Maybe I can help," said Max's mum. She climbed in beside Max and flicked a switch.

A red glow filled the water as the panels at the front of the sub radiated heat.

Lia grinned. "Wow! That's better!"

"Heated ice-breaking panels," said Max's mother. "After we faced Tragg the Ice Bear, I thought we needed something to deal with icebergs. Not bad for *technology*, huh?"

Lia shrugged, reluctantly. "I guess not."

"Final checks done," said Max, scanning the screens. "Let's hope she starts."

With the help of the Colossids they'd spent the best part of a day fixing up the

Leaping Dolphin on the Island of Illusion. As Max engaged the sub's engines, the hull thrummed into life and his mother grinned. "I never doubted us for a second," she said.

Max shivered. *Shame we haven't fixed the heating* inside *the sub!*

The *Leaping Dolphin* cut through the water, leaving the island and its strange inhabitants behind. The spider-like Colossids had been friendly in the end, but only after Max and the others had taken care of Cora Blackheart's latest Robobeast – Tragg the Ice Bear. Max's nerves were on edge. Cora was still out there, and the Lost Lagoon was dangerous enough without a pirate on the loose as well.

"Let's keep an eye on the long-range radar," said Max. "We don't want anyone sneaking up on us."

Max had always used to think the Lost Lagoon was a myth, like a lot of other seafarer's tales. That was, until they'd been sucked through some sort of dimensional whirlpool and trapped here. Now the only way to navigate out was to make a special compass using four rare metals. So far they had recovered two – a blue nugget of Galdium from an underwater volcano and a white Rullium sword from the Colossid armoury. Now they just needed some Fennum and some Barrum. *Two more metals to find in an uncharted sea...*

It wasn't going to be easy.

But if they failed, Cora Blackheart – the pirate even the worst pirates feared – might find her way back to the seas of Nemos. There was no telling what death and destruction she might bring with her Robobeasts.

We can't let that happen, thought Max.

"You look worried," said his mother.

Her words snapped Max from his thoughts.

"Just wondering where we start," he said.

"We've found two metals already," said his mother. "We just need to keep looking."

Her eyes dropped, and Max realised that she was trying to put on a brave face. True, they'd found two, but they had no idea where to locate the others. Even the Colossids hadn't been able to help.

Max was about to turn away when his gaze snagged on the green brooch pinned to his mother's chest. It had been a gift from the ex-pirate Roger after the battle for Aquora. A green gemstone surrounded by silver. Max couldn't help thinking there was something odd about it. On the Island of Illusion, Cora had been very keen to get her hands on the brooch. And Max was sure that at one point, when his mother touched it, her eyes had turned the same green as the gemstone. But perhaps it was just the light reflecting…

"Where other metals, Max?" said Rivet. The dogbot was lying on the bottom of the sub, metal tail wagging.

"I don't know," said Max. "Maybe you can sniff them out, boy."

Rivet laid his head on the ground. "What they smell like, Max?"

"I don't know that either," said Max, allowing himself a smile. "I was only joking."

Leaving his mum with the controls, Max climbed out of his seat and went to the rear of the sub, where the two metals were stored. He opened the lid of a small container, and took out the blue nugget of Galdium. It was surprisingly dense – the lump was the size of his fist, but heavier than a wet sandbag.

The Rullium sword that rested beside the container couldn't have been more different. Max picked it up and swished it through the air like a feather, squinting at its dazzling blade. The Colossids were a warrior species, who loved to fight for honour in a combat arena. Their emperor had only given Max the sword after he had proved himself by defending them from Tragg the Ice Bear.

Max ran his finger along the flat side of the sword's blade. He expected it to be smooth, but to his surprise it wasn't. The metal was irregular – slightly bumpy from hilt to point. Perhaps it was just a flaw, or perhaps not…

"Hey, Mum?" he said. "Feel this."

He took the sword to her, and let her move the pad of her finger up and down the Rullium surface. "Maybe the bumps mean something?"

His mother frowned. "I guess so." She held the blade up to her eye level and looked along it. She shrugged. "None of us can read Colossid, though."

Max nodded, but a thought leaped into his

mind. He certainly couldn't read Colossid, but he knew someone who might be able to. "Wake up, Riv," he said.

His dogbot jumped to his feet, red eyes flashing. "Yes, Max?"

Max twisted the dogbot's ear to operate the language function, and made Rivet lay his paw on the blade.

"Translate, Riv," he said.

As Rivet's paw passed over the blade, an expressionless robotic voice spoke through his speakers.

"This is the sword of Callox, lieutenant of the Octopod Forces, who defeated twenty-three opponents in the arena, who defended the Island from attack by the Gelanoi, who led the forces of Anthrix II against the Grand Haruspix of Vek in the year..."

The list of achievements went on and on, naming species and places that Max had never been to or even heard of.

"All very interesting," said Max's mum, "but not much help. Good try, Max. We have the metal, that's what matters. What's written on it isn't important."

Max turned down Rivet's speakers.

"I guess you're right," he replied. It had

been worth a try.

"Fennum, Max!" said Rivet in his usual voice, eyes flashing. "Fennum!"

"What?" said Max and Niobe together.

Rivet went back to reading. "...who followed the ice-birds west, to the Fennum beacon, and there met the Breathless One."

Max punched the air. "Good work, Riv!"

Lia appeared at the watershield again. "What's going on in there?" she said through her headset communicator.

Max held the Rullium sword aloft. "We're going to follow the ice-birds west!" he said.

Lia frowned, looking confused.

"Never mind," said Max. "Let's just say we've got a lead."

As he jumped back into the sub's seat, Max tried not to think about who the "Breathless One" might be. Something told him he or she wouldn't be friendly...

CHAPTER TWO

THE ICE-BIRDS

As he altered the *Leaping Dolphin*'s course westward, Max told Lia about the message on the blade.

"Ever heard of ice-birds?" his mother asked.

The Merryn princess scowled and shook her head. Max couldn't help smiling to himself. Lia hated not knowing things about the ocean.

Max pushed the engines to full throttle and the sub shot through the sea. The temperature gauge on the control panel told him the exterior water temperature was dipping all the time, approaching freezing.

What better place to find "ice-birds" than above a frozen sea?

"Maybe we should head nearer the surface," he suggested.

"Good thinking," said his mother. "We can use the periscope to keep an eye out for anything in the air."

Max tugged back on the controls and the *Leaping Dolphin*'s nose came up, carrying them towards the surface. As the depth reading counted down, a sense of unease crept over Max's skin. Cora Blackheart probably had plenty of scanners which could pick them out underneath the water, but on the surface they'd be even more exposed. He turned a dial to extend the radar scope – if their enemy came for them, Max wanted to know a long time in advance.

Max slowed the sub and navigated between drifting icebergs as his mother activated the periscope. A screen above their heads flickered into life as the peri-cam broke the surface of the water.

At first all Max could make out were choppy waves and towering icebergs under a clear blue sky – frozen ocean as far as the eye could see. Lia leaped above the water on Spike, then went crashing underneath again with a huge splash.

"Careful!" said Max through the communicator. "Cora might be nearby."

Max let his free hand rest on Rivet's metal head for comfort.

"SANDWICHES!" said Rivet.

"Huh?" said Max.

"SANDWICHES!" said Rivet again.

"What's got into him?" said his mother.

Max concentrated on steering them between two icebergs. "His language function has always had bugs," he explained. "He once said nothing but 'Who's a pretty boy then?' for a week. Ignore him, I'll do a fix in a minute. Wait, what's that?"

He pointed to the corner of the peri-cam screen, where a dark shape flitted in the sky. His mother adjusted to track it. More shapes appeared.

"Birds!" said his mother. "Well spotted, Max! I'm magnifying now."

She squeezed the trigger on the control stick and the peri-cam zoomed. Sure enough, several huge, slender blue birds filled the sky. Their stiff, jagged feathers made them look like they were made from clusters of ice. Max checked their bearing and saw they were flocking west.

Ice-birds…

His mother gasped.

"What is it?" he asked.

She pointed at the screen. "The birds – they're scattering. Look!"

Max seized the controls and guided the sub towards the surface. The *Leaping Dolphin* rose above the waves and water receded down its front shield.

In the distance was a ship. Max could see that it looked ancient, like something from a storybook about the first seafarers. It was made of wooden timbers – a wide barge with a single mast and furled sail. There were several people on board, bare-chested and leaning over the rails.

"Breathers!" said Lia through her communicator. Max saw that just her head was poking above the surface and she'd donned her Amphibio mask.

The people seemed to have blue faces, and carried objects in their hands. Every so often one would hold up one of the objects, spinning it over their head. The birds in the sky were swooping back and forth in disarray. Max edged the *Leaping Dolphin* closer.

"They're using slingshots!" said his mother,

leaning out of her seat and squinting.

Max saw it too. A rock left the end of one of the spinning objects, and smacked right into a bird. Its wings folded and it plummeted towards the water.

"Brutes!" cried Lia. "We've got to stop them!"

Before Max could do or say anything, the Merryn girl was cutting through the water on Spike, silver hair trailing in the currents.

"Don't!" cried Max. He knew how much Lia hated any animal suffering, but they didn't know what they were dealing with yet.

"Stop!" shouted his mother.

Lia either didn't hear them, or chose to ignore their warnings. Max engaged the thrusters to pursue her, but he could see it was too late.

Spike jumped from the water, cutting the air with his sword. Lia gave a screeching cry and launched herself off the fish's back. As Spike plunged back into the water, Lia thumped straight into one of the Breathers, knocking the slingshot from his hand and sending them both tumbling out of sight across the deck.

Max killed the *Leaping Dolphin*'s engine and scrambled up the ladder towards the top hatch.

"Wait!" said his mother. "You'll get yourself killed!"

"I can't leave Lia," Max shot back. He opened the hatch and clambered out. They were only a few ship-lengths from the barge now and drifting closer by the second. The ice-birds had vanished, but there wasn't time to worry about that now. One of the Breathers saw him and raised his slingshot. Max dived off the sub, and the waters snatched him in a breath-stopping embrace. *By Thallos, it's cold!* He swam with powerful strokes towards the barge, passing Spike who was swimming in panicked circles around the boat.

Max broke the surface at the back end of the barge and dragged himself on board,

dripping wet. Several of the Breathers backed
away, jabbering to each other in a language
Max didn't know. Now Max could see them
better, he realised they'd painted their faces
blue in strange swirling patterns. Their hair
was wild and tangled and several had bits
of fish-bone jewellery piercing their lips or

noses. Those who weren't bare-chested had
tunics made of dried seaweed and threaded
pieces of wood. Their skirts were some sort
of woven matting.

Two of the crew – both men – had Lia
held between them. Her arms were pinned
behind her back, and above her Amphibio

mask her eyes were wide and fearful.

"Let her go, please!" said Max, gasping for breath after the hard swim. He held up both his hands, palms outward, hoping they understood he was no threat. One of the Breathers, a man with scars criss-crossing his chest and a particularly wide bone sticking through both cheeks, walked forwards slowly, eyes narrowed. He held a simple wooden spear with a wicked, sharp point, black where it had been hardened in a fire.

"She doesn't understand your ways," said Max, pointing to Lia. "The ice-birds are important to us."

When the stranger was a few metres away, he stopped. His eyes flicked slightly to Max's left and he nodded. Max heard the creak of a footstep just behind him, and spun around. Something lashed through the air at his head and he raised his hands.

He felt the thump of impact, then pain.

Then everything went black.

CHAPTER THREE

THE LOST CITY OF UR

When Max opened his eyes, just a crack, the light felt like a dagger piercing his temples. He was lying on his back. Cautiously, he rolled his head to one side. Through the blur of pain he saw Lia and his mother, both sitting on the floor with their hands tied together. A robotic whimper made him look the other way. They'd got Rivet too, trapped in a thick-corded net and hopelessly tangled, with his muzzle tied shut.

Max sat up, and found that his own hands and ankles were tied too. They were in a cavernous wooden hall, smelly and smoky, lit by dirty candles placed at intervals on the walls in holders. There didn't seem to be any chairs, but around the outside of the room Max saw piles of glinting metal and other scrap. Pieces of machinery, some quite old and rusted, were stacked with fragments of weaponry and ship-tech.

Max cast his eyes about, looking for an escape route, but the wooden double doors were guarded by two men with slingshots and spears. *I'll have to bide my time.*

His mother scrambled to her feet and began poking at the assorted rubbish with one boot, peering at things.

"Max?" said Lia. "Are you okay? I'm sorry, I... Perhaps I overreacted."

"Maybe a little," said Max.

"But they were killing those birds!" Lia protested.

There was a scraping sound, and Max saw that his mother was dragging an old-fashioned book out of the wreckage, using the sole of her boot.

"What have you found?" asked Max.

His mother kneeled down. "I'm not sure," she said. "But look at the cover."

The tattered leather-bound volume had a spider embossed on the cover.

"I wonder if it has something to do with the Colossids," she said.

"Maybe we should be trying to work out where we are," said Max, his frustration getting the better of him. "And how to get out of here."

Just then the doors opened again and a stream of men and women filed in. Max's mum pushed the book away and stood.

These people were dressed much more finely than the sailors who'd captured them. They wore polar bear fur, whale-skin pelts, and robes decorated with shining fish scales.

"Disgusting!" muttered Lia. "How could anyone..."

Max managed to catch her eye, and she stopped talking. *We really don't need to annoy these people any more.*

Many of the newcomers wore jewellery as well, gold and silver inlaid with precious stones of every colour. They murmured to each other under their breath, pointing at Max, Lia and his mother. One screamed in horror at the sight of Rivet, still tied up on the ground. Another brought out a knife, and cut the ropes tying their hands together.

A huge man stepped forward, laden with golden chains, every finger adorned with chunky rings. He even had jewels plaited into his beard. He threw his arms wide.

"We are the councillors of Ur," he announced.

"You speak Aquoran!" said Max's mother.

"Of course," the man replied. "We left the cities of the Delta Quadrant in search of a better life. A life without machines or technology. This wooden city – the city of Ur – is our home."

"But—" began Max.

"Silence!" snapped the big man. He turned to the others. "These invaders must be put to death to protect the secrecy of Ur."

Max did a double take as the words sank in. "What?"

The bearded man gave him a hard stare. "You will all be executed."

"Hold on!" said Max. "What about a fair trial?"

The man frowned. "You are spies, using our

waters without permission. Our way of life is everything to us. Your lives are nothing."

"What if we promise not to tell anyone?" said Lia. "You can't just kill us!"

One of the other councillors, a rake-thin woman in a dress of sealskin, walked forward. Her greedy eyes fixed on the green brooch.

"Perhaps, Olaf, we could take their word if they showed us a token of their honour. This pretty trinket would go some way."

Max's mother backed away.

"No!" said Max. He didn't know what was special about that brooch, but he couldn't just let them take it. Not without a fight.

"Be patient, Erika," said the bearded man. "You can strip them of whatever you wish when they are dead." He pointed with a gold-ringed finger. "Take them to the killing pool."

Max glanced at Lia and his mother. "I don't like the sound of that," he muttered.

"What about the robot?" asked another man wearing polar bear furs.

"Leave it here for now," said Olaf. "We can disassemble him later."

Rivet whimpered again.

"Don't you dare!" shouted Max, throwing himself at the Ur councillor. At once, the guards grabbed him and pulled him away.

The Councillors filed out of the room first, then the rest of the guards closed in, forcing Max and the others out at spear-point.

Outside, Max saw that the city really was made entirely of wood. Whereas Aquora bristled with gleaming needle-like skyscrapers rising up into the clouds, the tallest building Max could see here teetered four or five storeys high. There were wooden walls and walkways, sloping roofs

and jetties sticking out into the water.

Immediately ahead of them, two rows of people had formed, perhaps a hundred or more, each wielding a heavy wooden club. They spat and shouted wildly, but Max had no choice but to walk between them.

It can't end like this, he thought.

At the far end of the rows of Ur people was a wooden cage, its door open. Max was pushed inside along with his mother and Lia. The

door was slammed shut, and fastened using a wooden key.

The crowd fanned out and Max saw a hole in the ground, forming a circular pool of seawater surrounded by sharpened stakes. A simple A-frame crane and pulley stood beside it, and as he watched, one of the Ur-folk clambered on top of the cage and attached a rope from the crane to its top.

"Are they going to try and drown us?" whispered Lia. "They don't know we can breathe underwater!"

As one of the Ur-folk wound the pulley mechanism, the crane hoisted the cage off the ground. Max gripped the bars as it swayed in the air. Lia might be right, but if she was, it wouldn't be long before they came up with another method of execution. He struggled to keep his balance as the crane swung them out over the pool.

"Release the bonefish!" said Olaf.

The woman in the sealskin dress pulled a lever at one side of the pool and a hatch slid up. A dozen or so sleek silver shapes drifted into the pool, their bodies glinting as they rolled at the surface.

"Er…what's a bonefish supposed to be?" said Lia. "I've certainly never heard of them!"

Max noticed his mother's face had drained of blood.

"Th-they…they went extinct in our seas," she said, her voice tight with fear. "They're an ancient fish known for stripping flesh from bone. Hence the name. It was said they could turn any animal into nothing but a skeleton in seconds."

"Oh," said Lia. She looked like she wished she'd never asked.

"Lower the cage!" shouted Olaf menacingly. "It's feeding time!"

CHAPTER FOUR

FISH FOOD

As the cage was lowered towards the pool, the fish churned the water into froth. Max's mother gripped his hand tightly.

They're hungry! thought Max.

"There must be some way out!" said Lia. "If only we could stop the winch."

"Maybe I should have given that councillor the brooch," said Max's mother.

That's it! thought Max. Suddenly, he had remembered the moment with the Colossids on the Island of Illusion. His mother had just touched the gemstone and somehow that had made their enemies back away. "Mum, can I have the brooch?" he asked. "Quick!"

He held out his hand while his mother detached the gem from her suit. A fish leaped out of the water below, teeth snapping. Max took the brooch, squeezed it tightly in his fist and glared at the islander operating the crane winch, trying to concentrate on him as hard as he could.

"Stop!" he muttered.

Almost at once, a strange warmth spread through his hand, then up his wrist and arm. He felt it gather behind his eyes.

At that moment, the islander looked towards him and they locked stares.

Stop! Max screamed with his mind. The islander shook his head for a moment, then continued winding the lever slowly, but he was still looking at Max, transfixed.

"Oh!" Max heard his mother say.

"Max, your eyes have gone green!" said Lia.

Max felt as though the power was shooting from his eyes to the islander's.

STOP! he willed.

The cage jarred to a halt and a murmur went through the crowd assembled below.

"Did you do that?" said Lia.

Max kept staring. *Return the cage to land.* At once, the crane lurched, swinging the cage back away from the deadly pool until it was over dry land.

The crowd was shouting in disbelief. Finally, Max tore his gaze from the islander's. "The brooch controls minds," he said in triumph, as they hovered over the ground.

"Of course!" said his mother. "That must be why Cora wants it so—"

"What's that?" interrupted Lia.

Max turned and saw an ice-bird in the distance. *No, not an ice-bird. It's too big…*

As the creature flew closer, Max's eyes made out its monstrous shape. It was a bird – white-bellied – but it was huge. Wingtip to wingtip, it was at least as long as an Aquoran battleship, with a sharp yellow beak. Its wing feathers were white too, with black markings.

It was a giant albatross.

The bird wheeled once over the city, then dipped its head and swooped. As it closed on them, Max realised his worst fears had come true – the black markings were actually metal. "It's a Robobeast!" he shouted. "Cora's found us!" He turned to the islanders, cupped his

hands around his mouth and shouted, "Run, all of you!"

The Ur people froze as the giant bird's shadow swept towards the square. It opened its beak and the screech that cut through the air was enough to send several islanders to their knees. Max clamped his hands over his ears and watched in horror as twin gouts of fire burst from flame-throwers under each wing. The council chamber caught fire immediately, flames leaping up the walls and engulfing the building in thick smoke.

"No!" Max muttered. *The whole city is made of wood – it'll be destroyed in minutes!*

Cries of fear rose from all around the cage, and the islanders scattered among the nearby buildings. Only Olaf stood his ground, pointing into the sky. "Use your weapons!" he shouted. "Defend your city!"

As the Robobeast descended again, a few

islanders hurled rocks from their slingshots, but they bounced harmlessly off the giant bird's feathers. More flames spurted over the wooden buildings, setting them on fire.

"Get water!" yelled Erika.

Chaos descended on the square as the islanders ran back and forth, bringing pails and buckets full of water to put out the flames. Meanwhile the strange bird flew back and forth, setting more and more buildings ablaze. Max scanned it for robotics. Apart from the weapons beneath its wings, Max couldn't see any other modifications.

"How's Cora controlling it?" he said.

"Never mind that – focus on the winch," said his mother. "Get us down to the ground!"

But as Max turned, he saw that the crane operator had fled.

He felt a tugging at his wrist and Lia grabbed the brooch. "Give it to me," she said.

"I've got an idea!" Max watched, puzzled, as she angled the brooch into the sunlight. As the huge bird turned, light dazzled its beady black eyes. It twitched and veered away.

"Good work!" said Max.

Lia tracked the bird, keeping the rays of light directed into its eyes. Cocking its head, the Robobeast finally spotted them. Opening its mouth in an irritated hiss, it flapped powerfully towards them.

"Stop!" said Max's mother. "You're making it angry!"

"That's the plan," said Lia.

"What's the plan?" said Max.

The massive albatross soared low over the burning buildings, heading right for them. Max saw the twin barrels of its flame-throwers glowing blue with gas. But Lia kept angling the light into the Robobeast's eyes.

"It's going to fry us!" said Max's mother.

"Get ready to duck," said Lia.

"Wait!" said Max. "I think I get it..."

The Robobeast went into a glide, filling the sky above them.

"Now!" said Lia.

Max crouched beside his mother, just avoiding a blast of heat directly overhead.

The air filled with even more smoke. He felt his hair crackle and his skin bake. He watched the huge mass of the bird fly overhead, the draught from its feathers rocking the cage. The top of the wooden cage was on fire, and so was the rope attaching them to the crane. The next moment they were falling.

THUMP!

The cage hit the ground and opened, depositing them in the abandoned square. Max rolled away from the flaming debris.

None of the islanders paid them the slightest bit of attention. Most were black-faced from the smoke and ash, trying to rescue things from burning buildings or forming lines to tackle the blaze.

"We need to get back to the sea!" said Lia.

"First we find Riv," said Max, sprinting to the longhouse. One of the doors was already hanging off its hinges, damaged by fire. Max pushed his way inside, holding his breath against the thick smoke and keeping low to the ground. He found Rivet still tied up.

The knots were too tight to loosen, so Max searched through the smoke for something to cut them. His mother was rooting amongst the junk as well, he noticed. "This is no time for scavenging," he said. "Go! I'll meet you back at the *Leaping Dolphin*."

His mother grabbed something from the floor, then tossed Max a rusty hyperblade. "Use this!" she said. Max caught the blade and hacked through the ropes on the dogbot's muzzle and legs. Rivet scrambled upright.

"SANDWICHES!" barked Rivet.

Choked on smoke, Max staggered towards the door, where Lia and his mother were waiting. Niobe carried the leather-bound book that she'd been looking at earlier.

What does she want that for?

As they ran towards the docks, Max spotted the giant albatross soaring a short distance away. It seemed to have stopped blasting fire and was simply surveying the carnage below. *It must be looking for us*, thought Max. Cora probably had a camera linked up somewhere on its body. But how close was she?

The *Leaping Dolphin* was docked in the shallows, ropes trailing from its hull, tied to wooden mooring posts on a jetty. Max unlooped them and he and Lia jumped into the water, swimming hard towards the hatch. As he reached it, he realised his mother was still crouching on the dock, loading the book into Rivet's watertight storage compartment.

"Hurry up!" called Max.

His mother slammed Rivet's panel shut and stood up, just as Olaf appeared, clutching a long spear. "You're not going anywhere!" he snarled. He jerked his head towards the circling Robobeast. "You brought that thing here to destroy our city!"

"SANDWICHES!" barked Rivet, jumping up and gripping the end of the spear between his jaws. There was a crunch as he snapped the weapon in two. Olaf lurched away with a cry of panic, teetering for a moment on the edge of the jetty, arms wheeling for balance. Then Spike jumped from the water, his sword hooking the councillor's belt and tugging him backwards. The water swallowed Olaf with a splash, and a moment later he came up flailing and spluttering.

"Thanks, Spike!" said Max's mother, before leaping into the water as well. Rivet followed her, front paws first, in a perfect dive. Soon they were all clambering on board the sub.

Max jumped behind the controls and wasted no time steering the *Leaping Dolphin* away from the burning city of Ur.

CHAPTER FIVE

THE LIGHTHOUSE

A few hundred paces from the shore, Max slowed the engines and brought the nose of the sub around. His breathing had almost returned to normal.

"We did it!" said Lia.

"We survived," said Max. "But there's still a Robobeast on the loose! And we're no closer to finding the Fennum lighthouse."

"Or maybe we are," said Max's mum.

She was hunched over a control panel at

the back of the sub, flicking through the pages of the old book.

Max jumped out from the seat and joined his mother. Lia came too, with Rivet at her heels. Max saw at once that the pages of the book were blank. He turned one of the thick parchment leaves, then another. All the pages were the same.

"Great!" said Lia. "Very helpful. Who bothers making a book look so nice without anything useful inside it?"

But Max caught the smile at the corner of his mother's lips. He laid a hand on the cover, beneath the small picture of the spider, and felt the bumpy surface beneath his fingertips. *Of course!* "Riv, give me your paw," he said.

His dogbot crouched on its hind legs and offered up a paw. Max held it over the cover of the book, and turned Rivet's ear dial. "Translate," he said.

"*The logbook of Callox the Adventurer*," Rivet read.

"It's more Colossid writing!" said Max, his heart filling with hope. "And even better, it belongs to Callox. Maybe it'll tell us the way to the lighthouse. Lia, turn the pages. Riv, you translate!"

Max took a seat beside his mother as Rivet scanned the pages quickly, searching for a mention of the Fennum lighthouse. It wasn't long before they found the right section. Moments later, Max was piloting the sub on a new bearing, with Spike cutting through the water just ahead.

"*I followed the windward coast of the wooden island,*" read Rivet. "*When the seabed dropped away into mighty underwater cliffs, I plotted my course due west once more…*"

Max switched on the *Leaping Dolphin*'s scanners and sonar, mapping the way ahead. It wasn't like navigating with a proper chart, but it was the next best thing. They travelled on the surface, keeping a lookout for any sign of the Robobeast in the sky.

"*Mountains rose ahead, their flower-clad slopes descending to great depths. Here and there, their peaks broke the surface, forming small, uninhabitable islands..."*

Max steered the sub carefully between the peaks of the underwater mountain range. They were just as Callox described – covered in sea flowers of astonishing colours. Behind them, the island of Ur became smaller and smaller until it was just a grey smudge of smoke on the horizon.

"I hope they managed to put out the fires," said Lia quietly. "Even if they did try to kill us."

"Look!" said Max's mother, peering upwards through the domed watershield at the front of the sub. "Ice-birds!"

Max found himself grinning. A flock of the graceful blue birds were flying in a V formation directly overhead. He followed them with his eyes, then saw...

"Oh, wow!" he breathed.

Rising from the ocean, gleaming golden in

the sunlight, was a distant tall tower.

"The Fennum lighthouse!" said Max's mother.

"And even better," said Lia, "there's no sign of Cora or the Robobeast."

Max felt his grin slip away. If there was one thing he'd learned from his battles against Cora Blackheart, it was not to underestimate the pirate captain. She would find them – it was just a matter of time.

"Let's stay cautious," he said.

He set the thrusters to full power and adjusted the sub's course, gunning straight for the looming tower. The ice-birds kept pace, flying straight towards the same destination. As the *Leaping Dolphin* approached, Max saw that the lighthouse was standing on a small outcrop of rock. There was something familiar about the lighthouse, but it was only when they were close that he realised what it

was – it looked just like one of the towers of the palace in Sumara.

"Don't you think it looks a bit Merryn?" he said to Lia.

She frowned. "Maybe," she said, "but we build with coral, not Fennum."

"Well, we just need to get a piece of it," said Max's mother. "I'll find some tools."

Max let the sub drift up alongside the rocky platform, then engaged the dock clamps to keep it steady. His mother brought a toolbox from a compartment at the back of the sub. "Ready?" she said.

Max hesitated under the hatch. "Erm…do you think this seems a bit too easy?" he said.

"Come on," said Lia. "We're due some luck."

A gusting wind was blowing as they stepped through the hatch and onto the island. Max looked back the way they'd come, but the sky was clear. Up close, the tower rose at least twenty storeys in height. There was a small door at its base.

"You don't think someone actually lives

here, do you?" said Max.

"Only one way to find out," replied Lia through her Amphibio mask. She rapped on the door with her knuckles.

"It must be so lonely here," said Max's mother, glancing at the wide expanse of choppy ocean on every side. "It reminds me of my old island lab."

Over the howl of the wind, Max heard the sound of footsteps from inside. Then the door creaked open.

Standing on the other side was an old man, his wrinkled skin a pale lilac colour, with just a few silver hairs swept across his scalp. He wore a very basic-looking Amphibio mask, all pipes with a tiny whirring pump. The old man's watery eyes widened behind the visor as he took them in, and his mask pumped slightly faster.

"You're a Merryn!" said Lia.

Of course! thought Max. *The Breathless One!*

"I wasn't expecting visitors!" said the old Merryn in a voice that was little more than a dry croak.

"SANDWICHES!" said Rivet.

The old Merryn frowned. "What is that thing?" he asked.

Max held out his hand. "That's my dogbot, Rivet. I'm Max, and this is my mother, Niobe, and my friend, Lia."

The old Merryn shook Max's hand with his own webbed one.

"And you're Piscanias, aren't you?" said Lia.

Huh? thought Max. *How does she know his name?*

The old man narrowed his gaze at her suspiciously. "It's been a long time since anyone called me that," he said. "What do you want?"

"Can we come in?" said Max's mother, glancing nervously at the sky again. "It's cold out here."

The lighthouse keeper seemed to think

about it for a moment, then nodded briskly. "I suppose…if you must."

Max followed the old Merryn inside, still wondering how Lia knew his name. He found himself in a cosy, circular room filled with furniture sculpted from driftwood. The walls were covered with shells of every colour and shape. There were windows at irregular heights – small and round like portholes. And a spiral staircase made of coral rose from the centre of the room, up through the ceiling like a corkscrew.

"Take a seat," said the Merryn.

As they sat on one side of the room, their host went to a table and poured green liquid into four cups.

"You know this guy?" Max whispered to Lia.

"I might be old," said their host, "but I'm not deaf." He offered the cups on a tray.

"Seaweed juice is all I drink these days."

Lia took one and sipped. "Piscanias is the Merryn explorer I told you about before – the only one to have found his way out of the Lost Lagoon. I thought he'd died long ago!"

"Charming," said Piscanias. "I'm very much alive, thank you."

"Sorry," said Lia, grinning. "It's just – I recognise you from the old storybooks! I mean, when you disappeared, no one thought you might have come back to the Lost Lagoon."

"I always did like to leave people guessing," said Piscanius, smiling crookedly.

Max tasted his seaweed juice. It was good – much less salty than the kind they drank back in Sumara.

"This is a nice place," he said.

"It certainly is," said Piscanias. "Now let's get to the point, shall we? What are three strangers and a talking metal dog doing here in the Lost Lagoon?"

Max's mother set down her cup. She glanced quickly at Max, warning in her eyes. He knew what she was trying to tell him – *Let's not mention Cora and the Robobeasts.*

"We can see you're a man who values your privacy," she said to Piscanias. "We just want to get home, and we need some Fennum to do so – to make a compass like you did. Perhaps you could spare some?"

Piscanias peered over the rim of his cup, then shook his head. "I'm afraid I can't help you."

Max struggled to contain himself. "But… but this whole place is made of Fennum, isn't it?"

"It is," said Piscanias, "and I dredged the seas for every last scrap. The lighthouse is perfect. I don't intend to start chipping bits away to give to every Breather who walks through the door!" He sipped his drink then narrowed his eyes. "So if that's the reason you've come here, I'm afraid it's been a waste of your time."

CHAPTER SIX

A TRICKY MERRYN

Uncomfortable silence fell over the room.

"We could pay you," said Max's mother.

"No!" said Piscanias.

"Or trade something," said Max.

"I said 'no'!" snapped Piscanias.

Lia cleared her throat. "My father is King Salinus of Sumara," she said. "He could reward you with a title."

Piscanias stood and hurled his cup

angrily across the room. It smashed into
smithereens, staining the white wall a lurid
green. "Enough!" he said. "I don't want
your money or goods. I don't need a title.
I'm happy here, safe on land. Until today, I
lived in peace."

Max was beginning to think the long years of isolation might have affected the old man's brain. What sort of Merryn preferred living on land? But surely he'd hear reason. "Listen…" he began.

"No, *you* listen," said Piscanias, pointing at each of them in turn. "You're not touching my lighthouse. End of story. In fact, I'd like you all to leave."

He folded his arms across his chest.

"SANDWICHES!" said Rivet.

"Not now, Riv," said Max. He shared a glance with his companions. Piscanias wasn't going to budge – that much was clear. "We'd better go." *There must be somewhere else to find Fennum*, he told himself.

As they stood, a streak of something white splatted onto one of the windows, making them all jump.

Piscanias's face darkened. "Those filthy ice-birds!" he said. "Can't they just leave me alone? Always squawking and doing their business on my nice clean lighthouse."

An idea leaped into Max's head. "What if we got rid of them for you?" he asked. "Would you give us some Fennum then?"

Piscanias wagged his finger. "Good try, lad. I might have taken you up on that, if it weren't for a rather awkward fact. Ice-birds are attracted to Fennum, you see? Like flies to dung."

Lia snorted. "Pretty silly thing to build your lighthouse out of then, wasn't it?"

Piscanias glared at her. "Don't be smart, Princess What's-your-name."

"*Lia*," she snapped back.

"We'll try anyway," said Max, interrupting before things got too heated.

"Well, be my guests," said Piscanias. "It

won't work, though."

They headed outside, where the flock of ice-birds was circling. Max fiddled with Rivet's volume circuits, rerouting power to give them an extra boost. "Right, Riv – scare the birds, okay? The rest of you might want to cover your ears."

Rivet tipped back his head, and Max put his hands over his ears.

"SANDWICHES!" barked the dogbot as loudly as he could. "SANDWICHES! SANDWICHES!"

Max saw his mother and Lia wincing. But the birds just carried on swooping around the lighthouse.

"Told you," said Piscanias, leaning through the doorway. "Hopeless! And now I've got noise pollution too!"

"Maybe you can use your Aqua Powers," said Max's mother to Lia.

"Tried that too," muttered Piscanias. "Didn't work!" He ducked back inside as a splatter of ice-bird waste hit the door. When he came out again, he shook his fist at the sky. "I swear they're doing it on purpose!"

Lia had her eyes closed, jaw clenched. After a few seconds her shoulders sagged and she shook her head. "It's not working. Ever since we came to the Lost Lagoon I can't even feel my Aqua Powers any more. I hate this place!"

Max's mother leaned close to his ear. "Maybe we should use the mind-control brooch to get some Fennum," she whispered.

Max shook his head. "It's not right," he whispered back. "It's the same as taking it by force."

"Any other ideas?" his mother asked.

Before Max could reply, Lia walked right
up to Piscanias and jabbed a finger in his
chest. "You know what? You're nothing like
the stories. You're not brave and you're not
handsome. In fact, I think you might be

the grumpiest, most selfish Merryn I've ever met."

"Hmph!" said Piscanias. "I didn't invite you here, did I? You didn't have to come."

"But we did," said Max's mum. "We had to come because we need Fennum, badly."

Piscanias shrugged, backed inside the lighthouse and slammed the door.

"Great!" said Lia. "What an ungrateful old mollusc!"

A splash behind them made Max spin round. Spike was leaping out of the water in looping somersaults, throwing up spray and chirruping wildly.

"What's got into him?" asked Max's mother.

"Oh no... That!" said Lia, pointing into the distance where a huge shape rose above the horizon, giant wings rising and falling.

"SANDWICHES!" bellowed Rivet.

Max felt as though his feet were glued to the spot with terror.

Cora's Robobeast had found them.

And they were completely defenceless.

CHAPTER SEVEN

THE FLYING HORROR

"Into the sub!" said Max's mother.

Max tore his gaze from the giant albatross, but instead of running for the *Leaping Dolphin*, he pounded on the door of the lighthouse with his fists.

"Come on!" said Lia.

"I can't leave him in there," said Max. "What if that thing attacks the lighthouse?"

Lia sighed and banged her fists on the door as well. "Piscanias!"

"Go away!" came a voice from inside.

"You've got to come with us!" said Max. "You're in danger!"

"You don't seriously expect me to fall for that, do you?" came the answer. "I told you – it's a landlubber's life for me now."

A deafening screech sounded from the Robobeast's sharp beak, almost splitting Max's head in two.

The door opened, and Piscanias thrust out his head. "What in all the seven seas was that?" he said. Then his eyes found the approaching shape. "Oh, by Thallos! You brought that monster here, didn't you?"

"Er…well, it's complicated…" said Max.

Piscanias slammed the door shut.

The giant albatross was just a few seconds away, getting bigger all the time. Max wished he hadn't left his hyperblade on the sub, even though it would be next to useless against such a foe. Lia banged a hand against the lighthouse door, casting desperate glances back over her shoulder. "Let us in! Please!"

"Hide behind the lighthouse!" Max cried.

The three of them ran around the outside of the tower as the creature glided towards them, talons tearing through the air.

Ping! A rock bounced off the Robobeast's beak and it veered aside, rising up on a single strong wingbeat.

Max saw Lia holding a slingshot. "Good shot!" he said.

"Thanks," she said, with a grin. "I picked it up when we were fleeing Ur."

As the bird swooped past, Max saw there were more robotics – a box, a little bigger than a person's head, tucked close to its tail feathers on its back.

That must be the control hub, he thought. *But how can I possibly get to it?*

The Robobeast banked sharply and came round for another pass.

Lia was reloading.

"I thought you didn't approve of hunting birds with those things," said Max.

"I don't think that thing exactly counts as a bird," Lia said.

Ping! She scored another direct hit, making the Robobeast flap away.

The mighty albatross wheeled and descended, two hundred paces from the island, flying in a glide just a fraction above the waves. Orange fire was building in the depths of the cylinders beneath each wing.

"I'm not sure a stone is going to be much good against those flame-throwers," said Max.

"Back to the sub!" yelled his mother. "We're sitting ducks out here."

They sprinted towards the sub, where Rivet was already scrambling on board. Max's mother jumped through the hatch first, followed by Lia. Max looked back to see flames spurting from the cannon, dousing the lighthouse in fire. Orange tongues licked towards him just as he dropped into the hatch. Heat blasted over him, but he was safe as his feet hit the bottom of the craft.

"Descend!" he cried, tugging the hatch closed.

His mother sent the sub into a dive and water swamped over the front shield. Max's last sight was the Fennum lighthouse glowing more brightly than ever among the flames.

"I so prefer life underwater," said Lia. She was trembling slightly.

"What about Piscanias?" asked Max.

"He should be all right," said Niobe. "Fennum has a melting point close to three thousand degrees."

"But it will be like an oven in there," said Max. "We need to take out that Robobeast."

"How?" said Lia. "A hyperblade isn't going to have much more effect than a slingshot."

"Maybe we can build a torpedo launcher," said Max's mother. "If we adapt one of the thruster exhausts, it might work."

"SANDWICHES!" said Rivet, in a voice so loud it shook the walls of the vessel. Head ringing, Max adjusted the dogbot's volume back to normal.

"Good thinking, Mum. Let me see…"

Shhhrumm!

With a hissing sound, the water ahead turned to foam and something yellow shot towards them. A pressure surge gripped the vessel, and as the water cleared, fear turned Max's stomach. The giant bird was diving underwater, streaking towards them with its yellow beak gaping. Max caught a glimpse of a metal plaque hanging from the creature's neck. It read "HORVOS".

"It's coming straight at us!" said Max.

As the Robobeast broke through the water, driven by its powerful wings, the *Leaping Dolphin* rocked. The bird dwarfed the sub several times over. Max's mother jammed

the controls sideways to steer away, but it was too late and the beak closed over the front of the sub. The world turned upside down as the vessel flipped. Max slammed into the ceiling, then back to the floor, tangling with

Lia and Rivet. He saw his mother grab the controls with both hands.

In the chaos, Max scrambled across and slammed a palm down to activate the front thrusters, blasting super-heated water straight into the Robobeast's gaping mouth.

Horvos released them for a moment and the sub drifted, before being jerked around again. Max thumped into Lia and the two of them crashed into a wall.

Through the watershield, he saw a glimpse of the lighthouse.

That doesn't make sense...unless...

"We're out of the water!" cried Lia, finishing the thought for him.

Max gulped and steadied himself against the pilot's seat. Rivet was on his back, paws scrabbling in the air. Horvos had them dangling in its talons, as the lighthouse shrank below. Through the front screen,

Max saw the Robobeast's beak pointed straight ahead, its massive wings scything through the air. His stomach lurched as they climbed higher and higher, until the ocean was a plain blue canvas beneath them. They might as well have been a tiny crab clutched

by a seagull. Max had never felt so powerless. His mother was strapping herself into a seat, her face white.

"Where's it taking us?" said Lia, her voice just a terrified croak.

Max clung to the back of another seat. "To Cora, I guess."

Horvos tipped his left wing and the clouds wheeled around. In the distance, the lighthouse came back into view.

"We're turning," said Max's mother.

As they travelled towards the Fennum tower, the Robobeast began to slow and a horrible realisation dawned on Max.

"Oh no," he said. "Have you ever seen a seagull hunt?"

"What do you mean?" said Lia.

Max saw recognition in his mother's pale face.

"When they can't break shellfish open with

their beaks, they drop them from a great height – onto rocks," she explained.

Lia made a grimace. "And I suppose we're the shellfish, right?"

Max nodded, staring at the rocks far, far below. *There's no way we can survive a fall like that.*

"Maybe you're wrong," said Lia. But she didn't sound like she believed it.

A second later, right above the island, the talons released them.

Max's stomach lurched up towards his throat as the *Leaping Dolphin* plummeted through the air.

CHAPTER EIGHT

AERIAL BATTLE

"SANDWICHES?" barked Rivet.

Max felt almost weightless as they fell. Terror seemed to slow down time. He saw his mother scrambling at the controls, frantically pushing buttons. Lia's face twisted in fear.

He closed his eyes and waited for the impact, hoping it would be quick.

With a jolt, his feet left the ground then slammed down again. His head snapped back and he crumpled in a heap on the ceiling of the sub. It felt like some enormous hand had caught them in midair. Through the front shield, he saw they were still falling, but slowly now, drifting through the air.

"What on…"

His mother turned to him and wiped the sweat from her forehead. She was grinning. "Didn't I mention the EPS?"

"EPS?" said Lia.

"Emergency Parachute System."

"No, you didn't," said Max. "But I forgive you!"

"Why put a parachute on a submarine?" asked Lia. "Although I won't hold it against you either."

"I added it on the Island of Illusion," said Max's mother, "after those worms ate away at the ship and almost sent me to the bottom of the ocean. It's meant to slow descent to the seabed, but it seems to work out of water too."

The sub landed on the rock beside the lighthouse with a gentle thump, and Max peered through the hatch. The only creatures in the sky were the ice-birds. *No Horvos.* But he knew that Cora's Robobeast wouldn't give up that easily.

"It won't be long before it's back," said his mother. "Cora will want to scavenge any tech she can from the sub. Speaking of that, let's get working on a rocket launcher."

"We can't kill it!" said Lia. "It's only Cora who's making it behave like this."

Max stared at the ice-birds, a plan slowly forming. "Maybe we don't need a weapon after all," he said.

"You want to try and talk that giant Robobeast into not killing us?" said his mother.

Max smiled. "Lia's right. The key to defeating it is to dismantle the robotics – remove Cora's control over it. I think I saw something on its tail. If we can distract it with the ice-birds, maybe that will give me time to sabotage the tech."

"Two problems," said Lia. "First, my Aqua Powers don't work on the ice-birds. Second, how are you going to get anywhere near its tail?"

Max pointed to the brooch on his mother's

chest. "First, the brooch worked on the Colossids, so why not on the ice-birds? And second, I'll wait for Horvos to come to me!"

"Sounds risky," said his mother.

A screech cut through the ocean air. Max jerked his head around to see the Robobeast approaching at breakneck speed. His heart lurched. On the rocks, they were completely exposed.

"Any better ideas?" he said.

The ice-birds scattered from the lighthouse.

"I don't think we have a choice," admitted Lia.

Max's mother tossed the gemstone to Lia, who leaped up on top of the sub and started waving her arms.

"Come on…" Lia muttered. "Come to me!"

To Max's delight, the ice-birds stopped flocking away, and wheeled back towards them. Hundreds of birds descended until their blue feathers seemed to the fill the sky in a wave. They settled on the rocks just behind the landed *Dolphin*. Horvos swooped low again, black eyes focused on the sub.

It wants to carry us up again, Max thought. *And now the parachute's used up...*

"Wait for my signal!" he said, climbing on top of the sub's roof and waving his arms. "Come and get me, you oversized seagull!" he shouted.

Horvos flapped harder still, its reflection wobbling over the surface of the sea. Max planted his feet, trying to swallow his fear.

If this doesn't work, we're all finished.

The albatross closed at lightning speed. At twenty paces, Max cried out. "Release the birds!"

Lia's fist unclenched from around the brooch and the ice-birds sprang up in fear at

the oncoming giant. Horvos reared back in
sudden surprise at the rising swarm of wings
and beaks, screeching madly. Its talons raked
the air an arm's length from Max's face, but
he held his ground. As the Robobeast's wings
flapped in panic, Max threw himself off
the sub and onto its soft feathers. Then the

albatross began to climb and Max held on.

Cold wind whipped around his body, and his knuckles whitened in an effort to hold on. They flew straight up in jerking wingbeats, and Max watched the astonished faces of his mother and Lia drop below. If he fell now, he'd break every bone in his body. Fighting fear and gravity, Max hauled himself up the feathers on the Robobeast's back towards its tail. The huge bird hadn't even turned to look. *It doesn't know I'm here!* As they climbed towards the clouds, the ice-birds followed like an angry swarm. *Good thinking, Lia*, thought Max. *Keep it distracted.*

Horvos levelled out among the clouds, then circled, head cocked. Spotting the ice-birds, it wheeled round and blasted two spurts of flames. The flock parted and fell across the Robobeast's wings, raking with their sharp talons and beaks.

I haven't got long, thought Max, crouching beside the black control box. *They're more of a nuisance than a real threat.*

Sure enough, as he prised open the box, Horvos shook its wings and scattered the birds. More flame jets followed, blasting warm clouds of smoky air over Max as he worked.

The tech was straightforward. He just needed to unfasten it – somehow. He reached inside.

THUMP!

The tail feathers twitched like a bucking horse, almost throwing him off. Terror spiked Max's gut as his legs skittered off the side of the bird and dangled over empty air.

He plunged both hands into the bird's plumage and clung on for dear life. The Robobeast's head turned and one eye surveyed him coldly. *So much for not being spotted!* And there, under the iris, he caught sight of a camera, implanted deep in the cornea.

Cora was watching.

Summoning all his strength, Max hauled himself back onto the tail, which thrashed and jerked to throw him off. He plunged his hands into the wiring and gripped the cables.

The bird opened its beak to give a shrill cry, and at the same time Max tugged. The cry cut short as the black box and all its trailing wires tumbled free from the white feathers. Max watched it fall hundreds of feet into the sea below, to be swallowed by the waves.

"You've lost, Cora!" he shouted over the rush of wind.

The giant albatross opened its beak and let out a screech of sheer delight.

Horvos was free.

CHAPTER NINE

ONE MORE QUEST

The giant albatross descended smoothly towards the lighthouse, landing on the rocks with barely a jolt. Lia, Max's mother and Rivet all ran towards it, as the rest of the ice-birds gathered in its huge shadow.

"That was incredible!" said Max's mother. "I'm so proud of you, Max!"

Horvos extended a huge wing, and Max climbed down beside his dogbot. He was still shaking from the adrenaline.

"SANDWICHES!" said Rivet.

"You really have to fix that," said Lia.

Horvos surveyed them all with its huge black eyes, then lowered its body into a crouch.

"Goodbye!" said Max.

The bird pushed off from the ground, then climbed with steady wingbeats that

sent powerful draughts blasting over Max
and his companions. It reached the height of
the lighthouse, then turned and swept away
majestically.

"Hey, look!" shouted Lia, pointing.

The ice-birds were following, peeling away
from the rocks in unison, turning their bills
northwards. Soon all the birds were just little

dots in the sky far away.

Piscanias's head appeared at the door of the lighthouse. "Are you still here?" he said.

"The ice-birds have gone," said Max. "Now can you spare us some Fennum?"

The old looked up into the sky suspiciously, then a smile broke across his face. "So they have!" He quickly replaced his smile with a frown again. "But if I give you some Fennum, will you leave me in peace?"

Max nodded. "Deal."

Piscanias disappeared inside. They waited a few moments until he reappeared, carrying what looked like a small golden torch. "This flashlight is quite special – I made it from the very last of my Fennum supply," he said.

"Thank you," said Max. "But we still need to find Barrum. Do you know where we should look?"

The old Merryn cocked his head. "Maybe I

do," he said mischievously.

"And?" said Lia and Max at the same time.

A series of chattering squeals made them all turn around. Spike had his sword above the waves, waving madly out to sea.

"What's got into him?" asked Max.

Lia looked worried. "Maybe he can sense something?"

Max's skin crawled with dread. *Not another Robobeast…*

"Tell you what," said Piscanias. "I've got a telescope at the top of the lighthouse. You can see almost the entire Lagoon from up there!"

"Thank you," said Max.

"I'll stay in the sub and get working on the compass," said Max's mother. "We should have all the tools. When we do find the Barrum, we can just slot it into place."

Piscanius led them up the spiral staircase,

high into the lighthouse. "I don't come up here often!" he said, breathing heavily as he climbed. "It's not right for a Merryn to be too far from the water."

The top deck of the lighthouse had no windows, and in the centre was a telescope at least as long as Max was tall, mounted on a swivelling base with a built-in chair. It was made of Fennum too, marked with engravings and symbols in a language Max didn't know.

"I don't understand," said Lia. "How can we see anything from here?"

"Take a seat," said Piscanias, grinning.

As Max sank into the seat, the whole room seemed to tremble a little, and a crack of light appeared on the wall opposite. Slowly it widened, and the entire upper half of the roof rotated away like a boiled egg with its top cut off. A breeze ruffled Max's hair and clothes as he gazed out over a 360-degree vista of the ocean.

"Wow!" he managed to say.

He put his eye to the telescope, and turned the eyepiece to bring the view into focus.

Max had looked through telescopes on Aquora before, but this was something else.

He could see everything – the crests of the waves, even the odd fin breaking the surface. As he turned the telescope, the island of Ur jumped up before his eyes. He was relieved to see all the fires were out, even if many of the buildings were badly damaged. He even saw Olaf marching around, pointing and shouting. *No change there, then.*

He swung the telescope again and froze.

"Cora!" he muttered under his breath.

"What?" said Lia.

Cora Blackheart was riding Max's aquabike across the surface of the waves, fists clenched on the handlebars and hair billowing loose in the wind. She seemed to be looking right at him, straight into his eyes. But that was impossible, wasn't it? Her face was taut with anger.

No wonder, thought Max. *We've outsmarted her three times already on this Quest.*

It looked like Cora was alone. No sign of any Robobeast.

But she was closing fast.

What sort of trick was she planning this time?

Max pushed the telescope away and jumped up out of the seat. He looked at Lia.

"We need to get out of here," he said. "And quickly!"

Don't miss Max's next Sea Quest
adventure, when he faces

GUBBIX
THE POISON FISH

FREE COLLECTOR CARDS INSIDE!

COLLECT ALL THE BOOKS
IN SEA QUEST SERIES 4:
THE LOST LAGOON

978 1 40832 861 3

978 1 40832 863 7

978 1 40832 865 1

978 1 40832 867 5

OUT NOW!

Look out for all the books in
Sea Quest Series 5:

THE CHAOS QUADRANT

SYTHID THE SPIDER CRAB

BRUX THE TUSKED TERROR

VENOR THE SEA SCORPION

MONOTH THE SPIKED DESTROYER

OUT IN APRIL 2015!

Don't miss the
BRAND NEW
Special Bumper Edition:
DRAKKOS
THE OCEAN KING

978 1 40832 848 4

OUT IN NOVEMBER 2014

WIN AN EXCLUSIVE
GOODY BAG

In every Sea Quest book the Sea Quest logo is
hidden in one of the pictures. Find the logos in books
13-16, make a note of which pages they appear on and
go online to enter the competition at

www.seaquestbooks.co.uk

Each month we will put all of the correct entries into a draw
and select one winner to receive a special Sea Quest goody bag.

You can also send your entry on a postcard to:

Sea Quest Competition, Orchard Books,
338 Euston Road, London, NW1 3BH

Don't forget to include your name and address!

GOOD LUCK

Closing Date: Nov 30th 2014

DARE YOU DIVE IN?

Deep in the water lurks a new breed of Beast.

If you want the latest news and exclusive Sea Quest goodies, join our Sea Quest Club!

Visit www.seaquestbooks.co.uk/club and sign up today!

IF YOU LIKE SEA QUEST, YOU'LL LOVE BEAST QUEST!

Series 1: COLLECT THEM ALL!

An evil wizard has enchanted the magical beasts of Avantia. Only a true hero can free the beasts and save the land. Is Tom the hero Avantia has been waiting for?

978 1 84616 483 5

978 1 84616 482 8

978 1 84616 484 2

978 1 84616 486 6

978 1 84616 485 9

978 1 84616 487 3